SHEILA RAE, THE BRAVE

by Kevin Henkes

Greenwillow Books • New York

*The art was prepared as full-color
watercolor paintings combined with
a black pen-and-ink line.
The typeface is Weidemann Book.*

Library of Congress Cataloging-in-Publication Data

*Henkes, Kevin.
Sheila Rae, the brave.
"Greenwillow Books."
Summary: When brave Sheila Rae, who usually
looks out for her sister, Louise, becomes lost
and scared one day, Louise comes to the rescue.
[1. Sisters—Fiction.
2. Courage—Fiction] I. Title.
PZ7.H389Sh 1987 [E] 86-25761
ISBN 0-688-07155-4 (trade).
ISBN 0-688-07156-2 (lib. bdg.)
ISBN 0-688-14738-0 (pbk.)*

For Gretchen

Sheila Rae wasn't afraid of anything.

She wasn't afraid of the dark.

She wasn't afraid of thunder and lightning.

And she wasn't afraid of the big black dog
at the end of the block.

At dinner, Sheila Rae made believe that the cherries
in her fruit cocktail were the eyes of dead bears,
and she ate five of them.

At school, Sheila Rae giggled when the principal walked by.

And when her classmate Wendell stole her jump rope
during recess, Sheila Rae tied him up until the bell rang.
"I am very brave," Sheila Rae said, patting herself on
the back.

Sheila Rae stepped on every crack in the sidewalk without fear.

When her sister, Louise, said there was a monster in the closet, Sheila Rae attacked it.

And she rode her bicycle no-handed with her eyes closed.
"Yea! Yea! Sheila Rae!" her friends yelled,
clapping their hands.

One day, Sheila Rae decided to walk home
from school a new way. Louise was afraid to.
"You're too brave for me," Louise said.

"You're always such a scaredy-cat," Sheila Rae called.
"Am not," whispered Louise.

Sheila Rae started off, skipping.
"I am brave," she sang. "I am fearless."

She stepped on every crack.

She walked backwards with her eyes closed.

She growled at stray dogs,

and bared her teeth at stray cats.

And she pretended that the trees were evil creatures.
She climbed up them and broke their fingers off.
Snap, snap, snap.

Sheila Rae walked and walked.

She turned corners.

She crossed streets.

It suddenly occurred to Sheila Rae
that nothing looked familiar.

Sheila Rae heard frightening noises.
They sounded worse than thunder.

She thought horrible thoughts.
They were worse than anything she had ever imagined.
"I am brave," Sheila Rae tried to convince herself.
"I am fearless."

The sounds became more frightening.
The thoughts became more horrible.
Sheila Rae sat down on a rock and cried.
"Help," she sniffed.

She thought of her mother and her father and Louise.
"Mother! Father! Louise!" she cried.

"Here I am," a voice said.

"Louise!" Sheila Rae hugged her sister.
"We're lost," Sheila Rae said.
"No, we're not," said Louise. "I know the
   way home. Follow me!"

Louise stepped on every crack.

She walked backwards with her eyes closed.

She growled at stray dogs, and bared
her teeth at stray cats.

And she pretended that the trees were evil creatures.
She jumped up and broke their fingers off.
Snap, snap, snap.
Sheila Rae walked quietly behind her.

They walked and walked.

They crossed streets.

They turned corners.

Soon their house could be seen between the trees.
Sheila Rae grabbed Louise and dashed up the street.

When they reached their own yard and the gate
was closed behind them, Sheila Rae said,
"Louise, you are brave. You are fearless."

"We both are," said Louise.
And they walked backwards into the house
with their eyes closed.